Color With Omar
Spring Edition Coloring Book
Copyright

Created by: Omar Thomas & Sabrina Thomas
ISBN: 978-0-578-38016-2

For more information, follow Omar on social media:

facebook.com/ColorWithOmar

instagram.com/colorwithomar

THIS BOOK BELONGS TO:

_____

COLOR WITH OMAR: SPRING EDITION COLORING BOOK

BY OMAR THOMAS & SABRINA THOMAS

ABOUT OMAR

Omar Tyrese Thomas is a kind, funny, loving 21-year-old with Autism, Cerebral Palsy, and an Intellectual Disability who likes to color. The "Color with Omar" series of books will give you hours of coloring fun for kids as they go on a learning adventure with its creator, Omar.

Designed for children 3 years and up, the engaging illustrations are created to help you learn and get to know Omar. Jump right in and color Omar's journey. Omar hopes that every child will love coloring these pages as much as he did.

In the "Color with Omar" series you will have a coloring experience with different seasons and holidays. You also will learn Omar's favorite things and most treasured activities along the way.

Omar is currently in the 12th grade. When he is not coloring he loves to dance and spend time with his nephew, Kenzo. Also, while in and outside of school he participates in sports such as track, soccer and volleyball.

INTRODUCTION

Omar and I are excited that you decided to purchase this Spring Edition
of the Color With Omar coloring book series.

This coloring book is filled with spring coloring pages and will provide hours of fun.
Springtime is a beautiful time of the year and we have some creative illustrations
of spring flowers, animals, nature and activity pages and so much more..

SO CONTINUE ON THE JOURNEY AND COLOR WITH OMAR IN THIS SPRING EDITION.

8

LET'S COLOR SPRING!

TULIPS

SUNFLOWERS

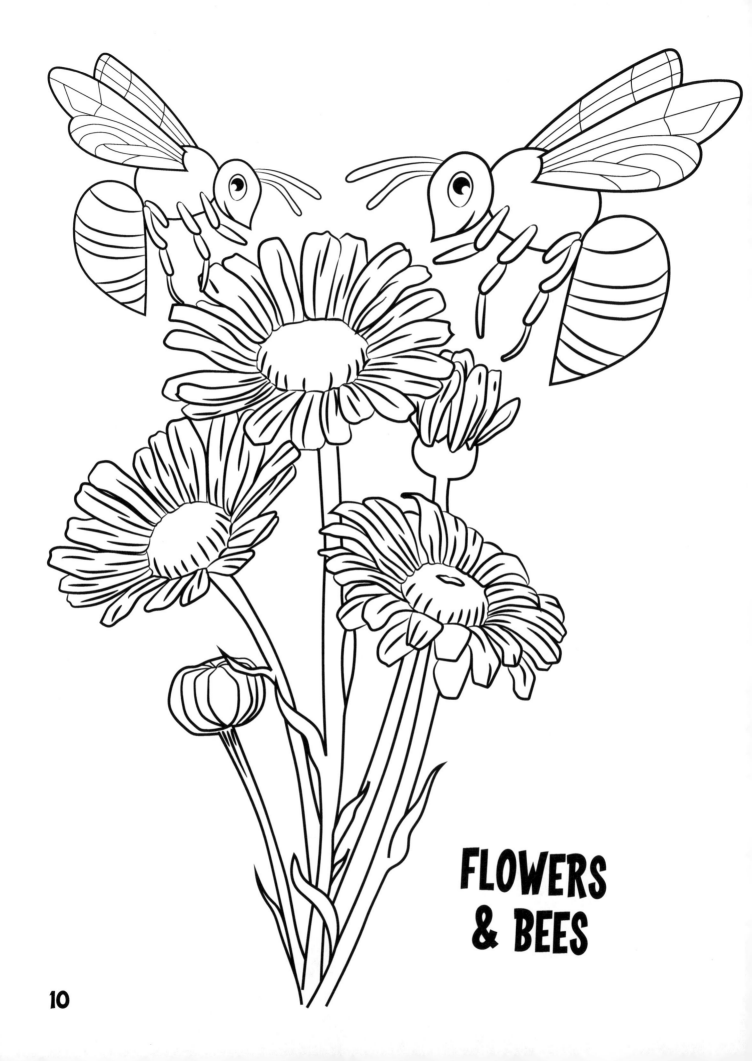

FLOWERS
& BEES

GARDEN

WATERING CAN

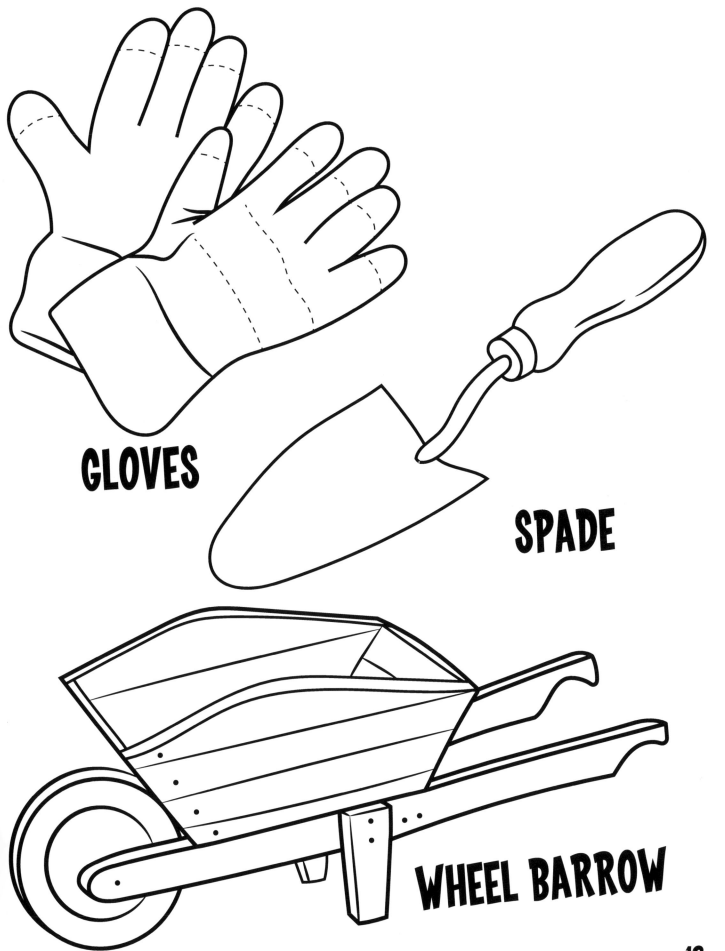

GLOVES

SPADE

WHEEL BARROW

TOMATOE

PEPPER

CARROT

14

WATERING MAZE

COLOR BY NUMBERS!

SPRING WORD SEARCH

```
S  P  S  L  T  R  J  B  K  X  I  G
E  X  P  S  U  N  O  N  Y  W  A  F
V  K  R  P  V  F  L  O  W  E  R  N
S  X  I  W  M  E  A  H  Y  T  J  V
J  O  N  Z  F  M  V  M  E  G  G  P
Y  H  G  N  E  T  L  I  H  L  T  L
M  W  E  I  A  U  R  A  I  N  M  K
B  E  B  Z  B  I  R  D  B  U  D  C
```

Find the following words in the puzzle.
Words are hidden → and ↓ .

BIRD   FLOWER   SPRING
BUD   NET   SUN
EGG   RAIN

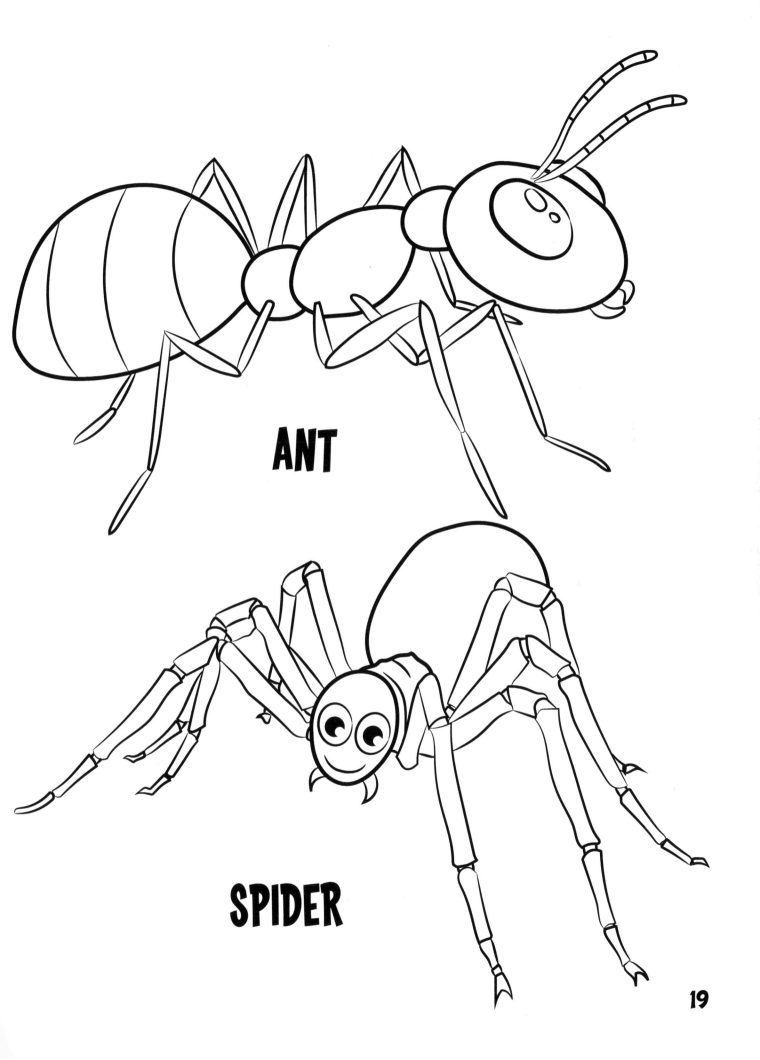

ANT

SPIDER

19

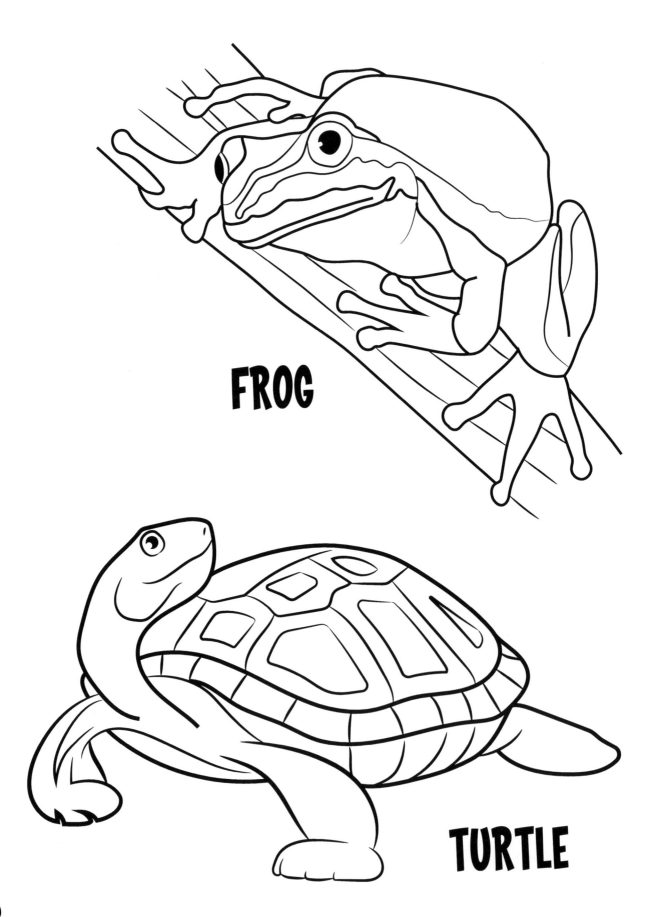

FROG

TURTLE

BUTTERFLY

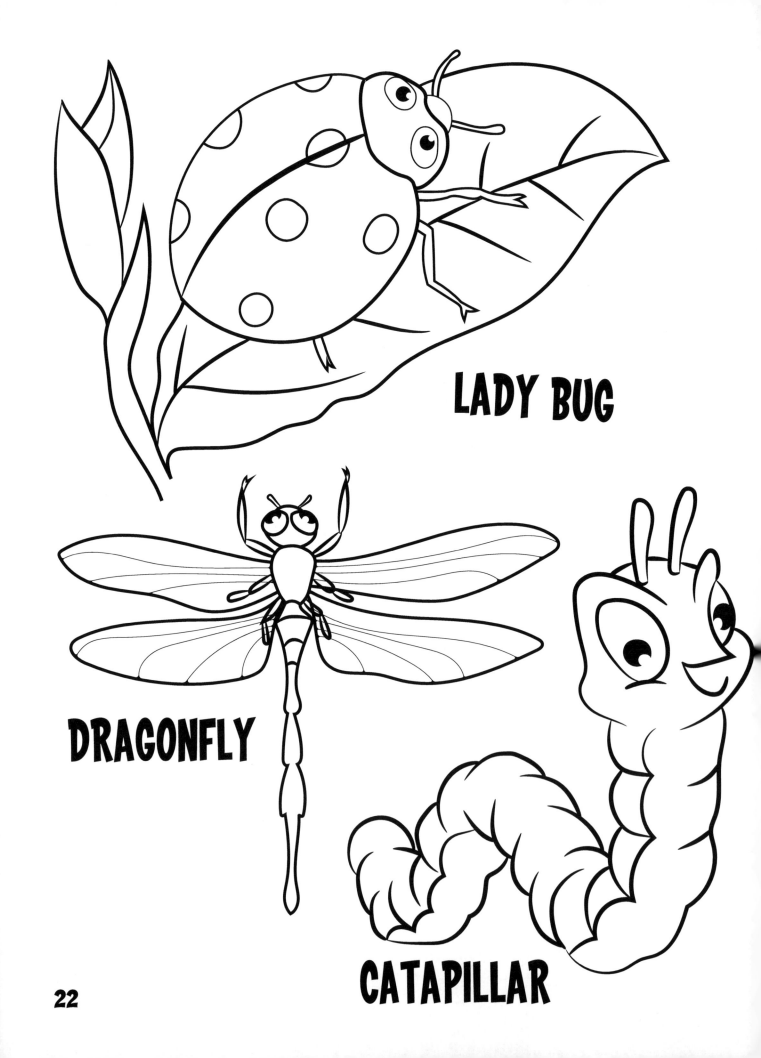

LADY BUG

DRAGONFLY

CATAPILLAR

BIRDHOUSE

BIRDS

COLOR BY NUMBERS!

INSECT WORD SEARCH

```
O  L  F  N  N  R  B  E  E  A  P  B
G  A  L  H  Q  W  O  R  M  L  Z  E
Q  D  Y  N  I  L  O  H  V  J  Q  Q
T  Y  B  M  I  I  D  S  C  W  Q  T
D  B  U  T  T  E  R  F  L  Y  Y  Y
N  U  E  V  F  A  G  Q  A  E  E  Y
K  G  A  M  O  S  Q  U  I  T  O  U
L  A  N  T  V  G  H  U  J  T  D  U
```

Find the following words in the puzzle.
Words are hidden → and ↓ .

ANT
BEE
BUTTERFLY

FLY
LADYBUG
MOSQUITO

WORM

LADYBUG MAZE

NAME ....

26

RAINCOAT

RAIN BOOTS

UMBRELLA

COLOR BY NUMBERS!

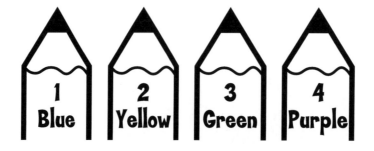

1 Blue	2 Yellow	3 Green	4 Purple

COLOR BY NUMBERS!

APRIL
WORD SEARCH

```
O T G R A S S M L D J U C A C H X F
J X S F T C M F C Z C S V G E S W Z
W O N F E K C Y I B M L V I X P F T
Z H Y I M F E Q G H H M X Y I R F R
N R N Y Q L N S F E X Q T C R I D F
W J O Q Q O R K I Y Q P C K A N S Q
V X P P Y W U T V J C N T W I G T Q
N R K B F E N E E K T K K A N T A S
V M J H O R P J I S T Q V R B R A K
K U Y A C S W J X J R V B M D O K N
D D H Z R Z P U D D L E S U N U N
Q D S K U J P D H B Q E O S G N X G
```

Find the following words in the puzzle.
Words are hidden → ↓ and ↘ .

FLOWERS   PUDDLE
GRASS   RAIN
MUD   SPRING
SUN
WARM

EASTER BUNNY

GRASS & SUN

RAINBOW

EARTH DAY

APRIL MAZE

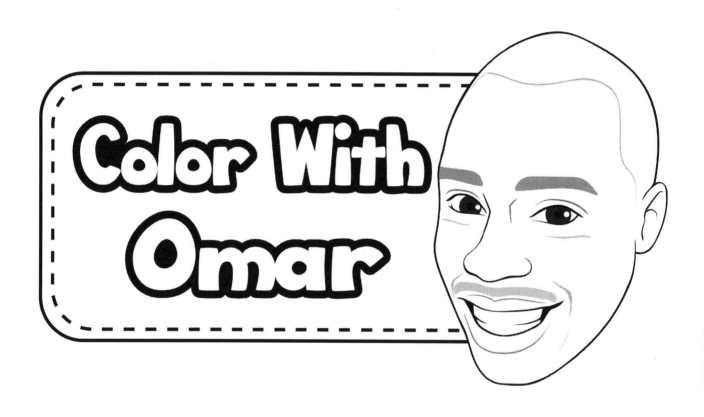

Color With Omar

Made in the USA
Middletown, DE
07 March 2022